Alfred Austin

Love's Widowhood and other Poems

Alfred Austin

Love's Widowhood and other Poems

ISBN/EAN: 9783337367213

Printed in Europe, USA, Canada, Australia, Japan

Cover: Foto ©Andreas Hilbeck / pixelio.de

More available books at **www.hansebooks.com**

LOVE'S WIDOWHOOD

AND OTHER POEMS

BY

ALFRED AUSTIN

London

MACMILLAN AND CO.

AND NEW YORK

1889

CONTENTS

CONTENTS

DEDICATION

TO LADY WINDSOR

I

WHERE violets blue to olives gray
　From furrows brown lift laughing eyes,
And silvery Mensola sings its way
Through terraced slopes, nor seeks to stay,
　But onward and downward leaps and flies ;

II

Where vines, just newly burgeoned, link
　Their hands to join the dance of Spring,
Green lizards glisten from cleft and chink,
And almond blossoms rosy pink
　Cluster and perch, ere taking wing ;

III

Where over strips of emerald wheat
   Glimmer red peach and snowy pear,
And nightingales all day long repeat
Their love-song, not less glad than sweet,
   They chant in sorrow and gloom elsewhere;

IV

Where, as the mid-day belfries peal,
   The peasant halts beside his steer,
And, while he muncheth his homely meal,
The swelling tulips blush to feel
   The amorous currents of the year;

V

Where purple iris-banners scale
   Defending wall and crumbling ledge,
And virgin windflowers, lithe and frail,
Now mantling red, now trembling pale,
   Peep out from furrow and hide in hedge;

DEDICATION

VI

Where with loud song the labourer tells
  His love to maiden loitering nigh,
And in the fig-tree's wakening cells
The honeyed sweetness swarms and swells,
  And mountains prop the spacious sky;

VII

Where April-daring roses blow
  From sunny wall and sheltered bower,
And Arno flushes with melted snow,
And Florence glittering down below
  Peoples the air with dome and tower;—

VIII

How sweet, when vernal thoughts once more
  Uncoil them in one's veins, and urge
My feet to fly, my wings to soar,
And, hastening downward to the shore,
  I spurn the sand and skim the surge,

IX

And, never lingering by the way,
   But hastening on past candid lakes,
Mysterious mountains grim and gray,
Past pine woods dark, and bounding spray
   White as its far-off parent flakes ;

X

And thence from Alp's unfurrowed snow,
   By Apennine's relenting slope,
Zigzagging downward smooth and slow
To where, all flushed with the morning glow,
   Valdarno keeps its pledge with hope ;

XI

And then,—the end, the longed-for end !
   Climbing the hill I oft have clomb,
Down which Mugello's waters wend,
Again, dear hospitable friend,
   To find You in your Tuscan home.

XII

You, with your kind lord, standing there,
  Crowning the morn with youth and grace,
And radiant smiles that reach me ere
Our hands can touch, and Florence fair
  Seems fairer in your comely face.

XIII

Behind you, Phyllis, mother's pet,
  Your gift unto the Future, stands,
Dimpling your skirt, uncertain yet
If she recalls or I forget,
  With violets fresh in both her hands.

XIV

And next, his eyes and cheeks aflame,
  See Other with his sword arrive ;
Other, who thus recalls the name,
May he some day renew the fame
  And feats, who boasts the blood, of Clive.[1]

[1] *Fifth in male descent from the Founder of our Indian Empire.*

XV

How sweet ! how fair !   From vale to crest,
  Come wafts of song and waves of scent,
Whose sensuous beauty in the breast
Might haply breed a vague unrest,
  Did not your presence bring content.

XVI

For you, not tender more than true,
  Blend Northern worth with Southern grace ;
And sure Boccaccio never drew
A being so designed as you
  To be the Genius of the place.

XVII

But whether among Tuscan flowers
  You dwell, fair English flower, or where
Saint Fagan lifts its feudal towers,
Or Hewell from ancestral bowers
  Riseth afresh, and yet more fair ;

XVIII

Still may your portals, eve or morn,
*   Fly open when they hear his name,*
Who, though indeed he would not scorn
Welcome from distant days unborn,
*   Prizes your friendship more than fame.*

SWINFORD OLD MANOR,
*   13th January 1889.*

The cottage where she dwelt was long and low,
With sloping red-tiled roof and gabled front,
And timbered eaves that broke the weather's brunt.
Ask you its age and date? None care I to know.
Save 'twas that goodly time which men call Long-ago.

Lene's Widowhood, Stanza XX.

LOVE'S WIDOWHOOD

I

Now I who oft have carolled of the Spring,
Must chant of Autumn and the dirgeful days ;
Of windless dawns enveiled in dewy haze,
Of cloistered evenings when no sweet birds sing,
But every note of joy hath trooped and taken wing.

II

But when I saw Her first, you scarce could say
If it were Summer still, or Autumn yet.
Rather it seemed as if the twain had met,
And, Summer being loth to go away,
Autumn retained its hand, and begged of it to stay.

B

III

The second bloom had come upon the rose,
Not, as in June, exultingly content
With its own loveliness, but meekly bent,
Pondering how beauty saddens to the close,
And fair decay consumes each hectic flower that blows.

IV

The traveller's-joy still journeyed in the hedge,
Nor yet to palsied gossamer had shrunk :
Green still the bracken round the beech-tree's trunk;
But loosestrife seeded by the river ledge,
And now and then a sigh came rippling through the
    sedge.

V

The white-cupped bindweed garlanded the lane,
Trying to make-believe the year was young.
Withal, hard-by, where it too clomb and clung,
The berried bryony began to wane,
And the wayfaring-tree showed many a russet stain.

VI

'There was a pensive patience in the air,
As sweet as sad, when sadness doth but flow
From generous grief, and not for selfish woe :
Such as can make the wrinkled forehead fair,
And sheds a halo round love's slowly-silvering hair.

VII

And such She seemed. The summer in her mien
Had something too of autumn's mellower tone ;
A something that was more surmised than shown,
As when, though distant woodlands still are green,
Embrowning shadows seem half stealing in between.

VIII

Then, in that season, She alone with me,
As when the world was virginal and young,
Went wandering slowly, pathlessly, among
Fair scenes it made you happy but to see,
And wish that as they were they ever still might be.

IX

Sometimes we lingered at a rustic seat,
To listen to the soothing music made
By uninstructed breezes as they played
Upon the mellow pipes of waving wheat,
Nor spake, but only smiled, the music was so sweet.

X

But when anew we thither came, we found
The swarthy reapers, like their sickles, bent
Among the stalks whose summer now was spent.
Soon the light swathes in heavy sheaves were bound,
And tawny tents of peace stood dotted o'er the ground.

XI

And when the hinds departed with their hooks,
And no rude voices hurt the silence there,
We to the spot together would repair,
And, carrying thither bread, and fruit, and books,
Make for ourselves a seat against the sheltering stooks.

XII

There would she read to me some simple tale
Of love and sorrow, which, being simply told,
And softly read, both saddened and consoled.
Whereat her voice would falter, cheek would pale,
And in her tender eyes the pity-drops prevail.

XIII

Oft would she bid me, when the light grew less,
Read or recite what poets weave in rhyme :
For verse, she said, doth not grow old with time,
And sheds a solemn glamour round distress,
Until grief almost seems akin to happiness.

XIV

When came the heavy slowly-creaking wain,
And, one by one the stooks being wheeled away,
There now seemed nothing there but yesterday,
Onward we wandered over stubbled plain,
Till rows of ripened hop replaced the garnered grain.

XV

There for awhile it pleasant was to lean
Against some time-warped gate, and watch the folk,
Whose gay patched garb their lowliness bespoke,
Stripping the fruitage from the alleys green,
While children romped or slept amid the busy scene.

XVI

Then did the sickle of the harvest moon
Its curve complete, and round itself with light,
Rising at sunset to retard the night.
Thrice thus it came, nor later nor more soon,
And thrice I hailed its disc, and begged of it a boon.

XVII

"O mellow moon, moon of plump stacks, and boughs
Blooming with fruit more juicy than the Spring,
Thee will I worship, thee henceforth will sing,
If thou wilt only listen to my vows,
And grant my sobering heart a home and harvest
    spouse."

XVIII

For, in those wanderings ne'er to be forgot,
My heart went out to her and came not back :
So that a something now I seemed to lack
Whene'er I wandered where she wandered not,
That wizarded away enchantment from the spot.

XIX

But I the ferment in my day-dream chid,
And brooded on it with a silent breast.
So quietly love sat upon its nest,
That, though she was so near to it, she did
Not see nor yet surmise where it lay hushed and hid.

XX

The cottage where she dwelt was long and low,
With sloping red-tiled roof and gabled front,
And timbered eaves that broke the weather's brunt.
Ask you its age and date ? None cared to know,
Save 'twas that goodly time which men call Long-ago.

XXI

And each new generation, as it chose,
Added a dormer there, a gable here,
So had it grown more human year by year.
It had a look of ripeness and repose,
And up its kindly walls there clambered many a rose.

XXII

And sooth a constant smile it well might wear,
For on a garden ever did it gaze,
That still decoyed the sunshine's shifting rays,
And bloomed with flowers which brightened so the
    air,
That folks who passed would halt and wish their home
    was there.

XXIII

Old-fashioned balsams, snapdragons red and white,
In which the sedulous bees all day were throng,
Hastening from each, too busy to stay long;
Wise evening-primroses, that shun strong light,
But kindle with the stars and commerce with the night.

XXIV

Moon-daisies tall, and tufts of crimson phlox,
And dainty white anemones that bear
An eastern name, and eastern beauty wear ;
Lithe haughty lilies, homely-smelling stocks,
And sunflowers green and gold, and gorgeous holly-
       hocks.

XXV

In truth there is no flower nor leaf that breathes,
But found a hospitable shelter there,
Being fondly fostered, so that it was fair.
Near proud gladioli with formal sheaths,
Loose woodbine clomb and fell in long unfettered
       wreaths.

XXVI

Full many a flower there was you had not found, '
Save for the scent its modesty exhaled.
When noonday heat or gloaming dews.prevailed,
A fragrant freshness floated from the ground,
And smell of mignonette was everywhere around.

XXVII

Behind it was a pleasance free from weeds,
Where every household herb and tuber grew :
Kale of all kinds, bediamonded with dew,
Each quick green crop that quick green crop suc-
    ceeds,
And all nutritious plants that prosper for man's needs.

XXVIII

But here no less did flowers abound, with fruits
That in September are themselves like flowers :
Rows of sweet-pea and honeysuckle bowers ;
Red rustic apples, pears in russet suits,
And china-asters prim, and medlar's trailing shoots.

XXIX

There too grew southernwood, for courtship's aid,
And faithful lavender, one happy May
Brought from the garden of Anne Hathaway.
For human wants can thus be comely made,
And use with beauty dwell, unshamed and unafraid.

XXX

Beyond it was an orchard thick with trees,
Whose branches now were bowed down to the ground
By clustering pippins, juicy, plump and sound.
Where it was sweet to saunter at one's ease,
Screened from too sultry rays, or sheltered from the
      breeze.

XXXI

Beside it ran a long straight alley green,
Paven with turf and vaulted in with leaves ;
Whither, on idle mornings, restful eves,
You might repair, and, pacing all unseen,
Muse on twin life and death, and ponder what they
      mean.

XXXII

Now that with bulging sacks the farmer clomb
His oast-house steps, and corn-stacks clustered round,
And shrivelled bine lay twisted on the ground,
We less than hitherto were lured to roam,
But in that pleasance stayed, and lingered round her
      home :

XXXIII

Gathering the last ripe peaches on the wall,
Splitting the pears to see if they were fit
Yet to be stored ; or haply we would sit,
Watch the slow team returning to the stall,
Feel the soft shadows float, and hear the acorns fall.

XXXIV

It happed, one day, as we sat silent there,
Since silence seemed still sweeter than discourse,
My welling heart upbubbled from its source,
And I besought if she with me would share
The sweet sad load of life we all of us must bear.

XXXV

A something slumbering deep in her, slowly woke,
Then tranquilly she laid her hand on mine,
As though to hush, yet heal, me by that sign.
And, as her quiet voice the quiet broke,
It seemed as though it was grave Autumn's self that
    spoke.

XXXVI

" Of gifts, Love is the fairest, rarest, best,
And what you proudly give I cannot choose
But humbly take : 'twere vileness to refuse.
Giving, you grow no poorer, I more blest,
And that which I accept, by you is still possessed.

XXXVII

" For love, true love, doth give not that it may
In turn receive, only that it may give,
And on its careless lavishness doth live ;
Squandering itself, grows richer day by day,
Wealthiest in wealth when it hath given it all away.

XXXVIII

" And my, my love I carried not to mart,
In the fresh bloom and April of my days.
Rather the bloom was April's less than May's.
For though the Spring still carolled in my heart,
Summer's more steadfast thoughts had there begun
    to start.

XXXIX

"What then I gave I ne'er have taken back,
And so have not impoverishëd my life,
Nor set my present with my past at strife.
However long or lonely be the track,
Love strays not from its road nor faints beneath its
      pack.

XL

"Dead? Is he dead? how could he die, or be
Other than living unto love whose breath
Defends whate'er it breathes upon from death?
Therefore so long as *I* live, so must he,
Warmed by my warmth and fed by it perpetually.

XLI

"Change? Did he change? How could he
      change, or lose
The glory love once rayed around his hair?
The years have gone, the halo still is there.
There is no art like Love's, for it imbues
Its forms with lasting light and never-fading hues.

XLII

" Why doth he come not ?   Wherefore should he come,
Who never from my side can go away ?
His is the first face seen when dawns the day,
His the voice heard when birds sing or bees hum,
And his the presence felt when night is dark and
      dumb.

XLIII

" As I have loved, so surely you will love,
Drawn hither oft, and never here denied ;
Constant as, when all springtime hopes have died,
The low unanswered coo of woodland dove,
Though no thrush pipes below and no lark trills above.

XLIV

" And should you come, and should you care to hear
I in some timely hour will tell you more
Of my Love's Widowhood, never told before.
The tale will fall upon a kindred ear,
And with its sadness suit the autumn of the year."

XLV

So nowise less I thitherward was drawn,
Crossing at will her threshold late and soon,
But oftenest in the slanting afternoon,
When lay the long grave shadows on the lawn,
Lingering till gleamed the star that hails both dark
      and dawn.

XLVI

But since there something was to say, unsaid,
And time for saying it had come not yet,
We mostly now, as when we first had met,
Would saunter forth with desultory tread,
And roam where winding lane or alleyed coppice led.

XLVII

Sometimes we brought our simple childhood back
By gathering blackberries, now purpling fast ;
Playing at which of us should show at last
The largest store, and ripest, and most black ;
Then, serious grown once more, we took our home-
      ward track.

XLVIII

Anon it pleased our fancy to explore
The hedgerow banks for some belated flower
That comes in flocks in April's magic hour ;
Primrose, or vetch, or violet, that wore
The smile of bygone days, or omened those before.

XLIX

These having found, and with them one wild rose,
That wafted back the scent of summer days,
And shamed the bramble with its lovelier gaze,
I made a posy fresh and young as those
That children carry home when ladysmocks unclose ;

L

Protesting love and beauty grow not old,
And in November twilight throstles sing.
" 'Tis only Autumn dreaming of the Spring,
That soon must wake to Winter's clammy cold,"
She answered me, as one whom sadness best consoled.

C

LI

"Gather me seasonable blooms," she said,
"For autumn flowers befit an autumn heart.
They do not mean to linger, but depart.
See ! the bur-marigold now droops its head,
And scabious withered stoops, slow tottering toward
    its bed.

LII

"Gather me these : I love each waning bloom ;
The berried bryony's discoloured bine,
The scarlet hips of scentless eglantine ;
The intrepid bramble, conscious of its doom,
That blends with fruit late flowers, to decorate its
    tomb.

LIII

"These to the tender heart are not less dear,
Because they mind of life's maturing debt.
Look where the honeysuckle lingers yet,
Curving its arm about the agèd year,
That gazes back its thanks through an autumnal tear."

LIV

When, on the morrow of that day, I went
Again to listen to her voice, she drew
Slowly my footsteps where no rude wind blew,
And, in the shelter of a leafy tent,
Her promised tale began, nor paused till it was spent.

LV

" It was the season when the bluebell takes
The place the waning primrose vacant leaves,
When whistling starlings build behind the eaves,
When in the drowsy hive the bee awakes,
When daisies fleck the meads and blackbirds throng
      the brakes :

LVI

" When wails the nightingale lest we be made,
Hearing the cuckoo's jocund note, too glad,
But even sadness is not wholly sad ;
When Hope shoots fresh to cover hopes decayed,
And young Love walks abroad, alone and unafraid :

LVII

"When dykes are silvery runnels that skip and sing
To flowers that lean and listen the whole day long,
And life is nourished but on scent and song.
Then was it that He came, and seemed to fling
A superadded spell and splendour round the Spring.

LVIII

"I loved him as one loves the music brought
By sylvan streams where other sound is none;
I loved him as one loves the lavish sun,
That scatters itself unbidden and unbought,
Or as one loves some great unmercenary thought.

LIX

"I was too buoyed on bliss that was, to deem
Of bane that might be; for the present gave
More than the past had ever dared to crave.
Onward I floated in a trustful dream,
Like one that sails adown some music-murmuring
stream.

LX

" But it was in no noonday dream I saw
A woman stand before me, calm and cold,
Like to those statues that men carved of old,
Majestic, abstract, without fleck or flaw,
That turn away from love, and dominate by awe.

LXI

" Her marble womb conceived him, and she claimed
His breath, and pulse, and will, as still her own ;
A being for her purpose got and grown,
As she wished wishing, aiming as she aimed,
And whom none else must touch, that wished to live
    unblamed.

LXII

" And when I pleaded vow, and faith, and trust,
She girded I had filched his troth by stealth,
And that I prized him, not for worth, but wealth :
With every cruel stroke and cynic thrust
Maiming Love's heavenward wing, to trail it in the
    dust.

LXIII

"Thereat I did not lower but raised my head,
And high my scorn towered up above her scorn.
'O woman surely not of woman born,
A woman shall redress this wrong,' I said:
'Keep what you claim as yours; your son I will not
    wed.'

LXIV

"And I have kept my pledge alike to both;
Gave what he asked, and what she banned withheld,
Love unrecanted, but my pride unquelled.
I scorned all bond save love's unwritten troth,
Trusting the living link engrafted on its growth.

LXV

"Nay, do not pity, or with pity blend
The frown that like a shadow still follows wrong.
Brief was the rapture, the repentance long.
When pride that soars hath towered but to descend,
Then humble duty proves life's only lasting friend.

LXVI

"But, while you blame, yet blame not overmuch,
Since 'twas not baseness which begot that fault.
Where prudence hesitates, I did not halt :
What marriage deems its own, I scorned to clutch,
And virgin kept my heart from every venal touch.

LXVII

"At least I loved : not loved as women do,
Who weigh their hearts in nicely-balanced scale,
Careful lest gift should over gain prevail ;
But no more dreaming those should bribe who woo,
Than ringdove in the copse that answers coo with coo.

LXVIII

"Nor did I mete out love as though it be
A thing to bear division, and to dole
In labelled fragments, body, heart, and soul ;
Withholding any of that triune three,
Yielding this one in full, and that but grudgingly.

LXIX

"Soul, heart, and body, we thus singly name,
Are not, in love, divisible and distinct,
But each with each inseparably linked.
  One is not honour, and the other shame,
But burn as closely fused as fuel, heat, and flame.

LXX

" They do not love who give the body and keep
The heart ungiven ; nor they who yield the soul,
And guard the body.   Love doth give the whole ;
  Its range being high as heaven, as ocean deep,
Wide as the realms of air or planet's curving sweep.

LXXI

" And thus it was I loved ; reserving not
One element of all Self has to give,
And in another's happiness did live ;
  Like to a flower that, rooted to one spot,
Yields sun and dew the scent that dew and sun begot.

LXXII

" Mourn not that love is blind.   If love could see,
Love then would scarce be love.   Its bandaged eyes
Gaze inward, and behold in clearest guise
The objects of its thought, which, since they be
Seen thus, appear more real than blurred reality.

LXXIII

" And Love surrenders not its dream even when
Life draws the curtain of its sleep, and cries,
' Awake ! behold the day with dreamless eyes !'
But wanders mournful 'mid the ways of men,
Missing the thing it seeks, nor hopes to find again.

LXXIV

" Thus can I never make a pact with life,
That strove to break my pact with love and death.
Nor shall I blame him ever with my breath,
And thus with blame set self with self at strife.
Enough, that he is wed, and I am not his wife.

LXXV

"There is an island off the Breton shore,
Small, and as simple as the lowly folk
From whose rude roofs upcurls the turf-fed smoke.
Sometimes the waves against it rage and roar,
Sometimes they kiss its feet, and woo it, and adore.

LXXVI

"Upon it is a little church-like shed,
Girt with a cluster of green nameless graves,
Green, but withal as billowy as the waves,
Yet just as motionless as those whose bed
Lies deep within, secure from trouble overhead.

LXXVII

"But one grave is there, shaped and smoothed
     with care,
That bears a name, engraven deep and plain,
On a small granite slab without a stain :
A name—no more—if fanciful, yet fair,
That looks up to the stars, and claimeth kindred there.

LXXVIII

" And in it do I often creep, and lie
Warm by my blossom that is cold within,
And faded ere it sorrow knew or sin.
Six summers did it gladden earth and sky
With carol and with song,—a bird, a butterfly.

LXXIX

" Then ceased both song and flight their brief
    sweet span,
And all my prayers, and tears, and kisses, then,
Could coax it not to kiss me back again,
Nor call life's hues to temples white and wan :
And from that hour it was Love's Widowhood began.

LXXX

" For while it frolicked in and out the door,
Or nestled in my lap, outworn with play,
I somehow felt He was not far away,
But might at any moment come once more,
And love and all things be as they had been before.

LXXXI

"Fondling its curls, I used to close mine eyes,
And dimly fancy I was fondling his ;
And when its little lips my lips did kiss,
My heart would swell, and then subside, with sighs,
And soul and senses float on murmured lullabies.

LXXXII

"But when its fairy form no more was blown
Along the wind, nor gleamed athwart the grass,
Nor longer in its little crib, alas !
Glowed like a moist musk-rosebud newly blown,
Then knew I, night and day would find me still alone.

LXXXIII

"There was a gentle venerable priest,
Who had loved it with a yearning ofttimes shown
By those that have no kindred of their own ;
A love that is by sense of want increased,
And felt the most by hearts that taste of it the least.

LXXXIV

"And piously he wept, and soothed my hand,
And oft besought, and aided, me to pray.
But since his sole joy now was ta'en away,
Shortly he followed it to death's dim land,
And he too sleeps in peace beside the Breton strand.

LXXXV

"None then were left who loved my blossom save
Two snowy-wimpled nuns, that, tender-eyed,
Smiled while it lived and sorrowed when it died.
But they were bidden elsewhere, and one lone grave
My sole companion now, with wailings of the wave.

LXXXVI

"Then with tears bitter as the salt sea-brine,
And which, like sea-mist, blotted out my gaze,
I came back to these quiet woodland ways,
Where, in my youth, I dreamed my dream divine,
And which must still remain for ever his and mine."

LXXXVII

She ceased : and I could hear a chestnut fall
From branch to branch, then drop upon the ground,
And in the slowly purpling air the sound
Of the first rooks returning to the Hall
From seaward marshy lands, and answering call with
      call.

LXXXVIII

Thuswise we listened ; neither having speech
To mate the silence.   But she knew my heart
Was nearer to her now, not more apart,
Since that sad story of the Breton beach,
And yearned still more toward hers, which still it
      could not reach.

LXXXIX

When next I thither bent my steps, I found
A something, heretofore I had not seen,
Almost akin to sunshine in her mien ;
A cheerful gravity that hovered round
The face of things, and drank content from sight and
      sound.

XC

"Welcome !" she said, "and welcome more to-day
Than ever yet, though welcome always here.
For we must do the service of the Year,
That kind taskmaster whom we both obey,
And whom we serve for love, whom others serve for
     pay.

XCI

" His need is very pressing, for behold !
The ruddy apples bend the branches down,
Like children tugging at their mother's gown.
There are all colours, russet, red, and gold,
Pippins of every sort, and codlins manifold.

XCII

" On their sweet pulp the thievish jackdaws browse,
And leave the half-pecked fruit upon the ground,
To nibble at the others plump and sound.
The wasps fall drowsy-drunk from off the boughs,
Or zigzag to their nests, to sleep off their carouse.

XCIII

" Look ! I have donned my apron with the hem
Of primrose tint to please your April taste,
And primrose-purfled basket.   Now, make haste,
And let us to the orchard,—branch and stem
Will soon be thick with thieves,—and be before with
    them.

XCIV

" Bring you the ladder from the lodge ; the crates
Are ranged already round the oldest trees.
Shall we not be as busy as the bees,
And gather yet more honey ?   Harvest waits,
And we, since hired, must stand not idle at the gates."

XCV

Thereon I did her errand, and we went,
With faces eager as our feet, to where
The juicy apples flavoured all the air ;
And, on a trunk the ladder having leant,
I swarmed into the boughs, contenting and content.

XCVI

And all the afternoon there did I pluck
The ripe and rounded fruit, and when mayhap
I found one lustrous fair, into her lap
I flung it down, exclaiming, " Bite and suck
Its sweetness with your own, and leave me half for
      luck."

XCVII

And so she did, not making kind unkind,
Or natural strange, by being grossly coy.
In all my life I never had such joy.
Like water wimpled by a sunlit wind,
I plain could see her face smile-dimpled by her mind.

XCVIII

Nor till the crimson-flushing sky o'erhead
Seemed to have caught the colour of the fruit
That lay in circles round each gnarlëd root,
    Stayed we our task; and then we turned our tread
Back to the porch, since there her homeward fancy
      led.

D

XCIX

She passed within, but I remained without ;
And slowly felt, as there I sate apart,
The pain that sometimes comes about the heart
When we have been too happy, and the doubt
If joy like that can last puts timid hope to rout.

C

Shortly I heard her voice, "Are you there?" she said,
And came and sate beside me.　From her face,
As from the sky the sunset light, all trace
Of late reflected happiness had fled,
And with a muffled voice she murmured, "He is dead."

CI

A letter lay upon her lap, but I
Looked not at it, nor her, but fixed my gaze,
As hers I knew was fixed, on far-off days,
When she was in her girlhood ; and the sky
Darkened, and one bright star beheld us from on high.

CII

I took her hand : she took it not away :
And in the twilight, which, when day is done,
Can make the past and present feel like one,
I found a free unfaltering voice to say
All that had filled my heart, full many an autumn day.

CIII

" He is not dead ; he lives ; he never died,
And never did desert you.   For you clung
Fast to his image, listened for his tongue,
Never a moment drifted from his side,
But shrined him in your heart, haloed and glorified

CIV

" Thus he you loved was loyal, trustful, true,
As man tenacious, tender as a maid,
And of no fate save infamy afraid.
Nay, he was leal and loving even as you,
And what in you were base, that baseness could not do.

CV

"Loving him, yet you thought of him as one
Who still would love you though you loved him not,
And would remember even if you forgot;
To be your shadow, needed not the sun,
But straight would hold his course, though hope of
      bourne was none.

CVI

"And such a one there is who loves you now,
And who will always love you, come what may.
Was it not therefore he you loved alway?
No new love this, only an ancient vow,
Mellowed to fruit which then was blossom on the
      bough.

CVII

"Sweet, dear! is youth, and sweet the days that bring
The wildwood's smile and cuckoo's wandering voice,
And all that bids us revel and rejoice.
But Autumn fosters, 'neath its folded wing,
A deeper love and joy than glimmer round the Spring."

CVIII

The silence moved not.   In the dewy air
The twilight deepened, and the stars came down,
And clustered round and round us like a crown.
I knew not if they circled here or there,
For Earth and Heaven were one, revolving everywhere.

CIX

I could not tell the sweetness from the smart,
Nor if the warm mist on my cheek were tears
From her loved lids or dewdrops from the Spheres.
There was no space for thought of things apart,
As her surrendered heart lay havened on my heart.

CX

And never again did gloom or cloud appear
While Autumn lingered in that happy land,
Where we still wandered, but now hand in hand ;
Watching the woodmen in the copses clear
Broad rings of space and close the cycle of the year.

CXI

But long before the ringing of the axe
Was hushed by silences of silvery frost,
The threshold of the village church we crossed,
And stood, with downcast eyes and bending backs,
Before a scroll that bore the twin words, *Lux et Pax*.

CXII

And children's hands had tenderly arrayed
Harvest Thanksgiving, that auspicious morn,
Round rail, and arch, and column ; blades of corn,
Garlands of rustic fruit, with leaves decayed,
And here and there a flower found in some sheltered
    glade.

CXIII

And children's voices shepherded the rite
That sanctified love's birth, and children strewed
Sweet-smelling herbs, thyme, box, and southernwood,
Under our feet, to augur us delight ;
And children's eyes they were that watched us fade
    from sight.

CXIV

And we are going to the Breton shore,
Together by a little grave to weep,
And place fresh flowers around an angel's sleep.
For I am living in her life before,
And She, she lives in mine, both now and evermore.

CXV

So I who oft have carolled of the Spring,
Now chant of Autumn and the fruitful days ;
Of windless dawns enveiled in dewy haze,
Of cloistered evenings when no loud birds sing,
But Love in silence broods, with fondly-folded wing.

A WINTRY PICTURE

Now where the bare sky spans the landscape bare,
Up long brown fallows creeps the slow brown team,
Scattering the seed-corn that must sleep and dream,
Till by Spring's carillon awakened there.
Ruffling the tangles of his thicket hair,
The stripling yokel steadies now the beam,
Now strides erect with cheeks that glow and gleam,
And whistles shrewdly to the spacious air.
Lured onward to the distance dim and blear,
The road crawls weary of the travelled miles :
The kine stand cowering in unmoving files ;
The shrewmouse rustles through the bracken sere ;
And, in the sculptured woodland's leafless aisles,
The robin chants the vespers of the year.

I CHIDE NOT AT THE SEASONS

I CHIDE not at the seasons, for if Spring
With backward look refuses to be fair,
My Love still more than April makes me sing,
And shows May blossom in the bleak March air.
Should Summer fail its tryst, or June delay
To wreathe my porch with roses red and pale,
Her breath is sweeter than the new-mown hay,
Her touch more clinging than the woodbine's trail.
Let Autumn like a spendthrift waste the year,
And reap no harvest save the fallen leaves,
My Love still ripeneth, though she grows not sere,
And smiles enthronèd on our piled-up sheaves.
And last, when miser Winter docks the days,
She warms my hearth and keeps my hopes ablaze.

A DIALOGUE AT FIESOLE

HE.

HALT here awhile.   That mossy-cushioned seat
Is for your queenliness a natural throne ;
As I am fitly couched on this low sward,
Here at your feet.

SHE.

    And I, in thought, at yours :
My adoration, deepest.

HE.

     Deep, so deep,
I have no thought wherewith to fathom it ;
Or, shall I say, no flight of song so high,
To reach the Heaven whence you look down on me,
My star, my far-off star !

SHE.

If far, yet fixed :
No shifting planet leaving you to seek
Where now it shines.

HE.

A little light, if near,
Glows livelier than the largest orb in Heaven.

SHE.

But little lights burn quickly out, and then,
Another must be kindled.   Stars gleam on,
Unreached, but unextinguished. . . . Now, the song.

HE.

Yes, yes, the song : your music to my verse.

SHE.

In this sequestered dimple of the hill,
Forgotten by the furrow, none will hear :
Only the nightingales, that misconceive
The mid-day darkness of the cypresses
For curtained night.

HE.

And they will hush to hear
A sudden singing sweeter than their own.
Delay not the enchantment, but begin.

SHE (*singing*).

If you were here, if you were here,
The cattle-bells would sound more clear ;
The cataracts would flash and leap
More silvery from steep to steep ;
The farewell of a rosier glow
Soften the summit of the snow ;
The valley take a tenderer green ;
In dewy gorge and dim ravine
The loving bramble-flowers embrace
The rough thorn with a gentler grace ;
The gentian open bluer eyes,
In bluer air, to bluer skies :
The frail anemone delay,
The jonquil hasten on its way,
The primrose linger past its time,
The violet prolong its prime ;
And every flower that seeks the light,
On Alpine lowland, Alpine height,

Wear April's smile without its tear,
If you were here ; if you were here !

If you were here, the Spring would wake
A fuller music in the brake.
The mottled misselthrush would pipe
A note more ringing, rich, and ripe ;
The whitethroat peer above its nest
With brighter eye and downier breast ;
The cuckoo greet the amorous year,
Chanting its joy without its jeer ;
The lark betroth the earth and sky
With peals of heavenlier minstrelsy ;
And every wildwood bird rejoice
On fleeter wing, with sweeter voice,
If you were here !

If you were here, I too should feel
The moisture of the Springtide steal
Along my veins, and rise and roll
Through every fibre of my soul.
In my live breast would melt the snow,
And all its channels flush and flow
With waves of life and streams of song,
Frozen and silent all too long.

A something in each wilding flower,
Something in every scented shower,
Something in flitting voice and wing,
Would drench my heart and bid me sing :
Not in this feeble halting note,
But, like the merle's exulting throat,
With carol full and carol clear,
If you were here, if you were here.

HE.

Hark ! How the hills have caught the strain, and seem
Loth to surrender it, and now enclose
Its cadence in the silence of their folds.
Still as you sang, the verses had the wing
Of that which buoyed them, and your aery voice
Lifted my drooping music from the ground.
Now that you cease, there is an empty nest,
From which the full-fledged melody hath flown.

SHE.

Dare I with you contend in metaphor,
It might not be so fanciful to show
That nest, and eggs, and music, all are yours.

But modesty in poets is too rare,
To be reproved for error.   Let me then
Be crowned full queen of song, albeit in sooth
I am but consort, owing my degree
To the real sceptred Sovereign at my side.
But now repay my music, and in kind.
Unfolding to my ear the youngest flower
Of song that seems to blossom all the year ;
" Delay not the enchantment, but begin."

HE (*reciting*).

Yet, you are here ; yes, you are here.
There's not a voice that wakes the year,
In vale frequented, upland lone,
But steals some sweetness from your own.
When dream and darkness have withdrawn,
I feel you in the freshening dawn :
You fill the noonday's hushed repose ;
You scent the dew of daylight's close.
The twilight whispers you are nigh ;
The stars announce you in the sky.
The moon, when most alone in space,
Fills all the heavens with your face.

In darkest hour of deepest night,
I see you with the spirit's sight ;
And slumber murmurs in my ear,
" Hush ! she is here.   Sleep ! she is here."

SHE.

Hark how you bare your secret when you sing !
Imagination's universal scope
Can swift endue this gray and shapeless world
With the designs and colour of the sky.
What want you with our fixed and lumpish forms,
You, unconditioned arbiter of air ?
" Yet, you are here ; yes, you are here."   The span
Of nimble fancy leaps the interval,
And brings the distant nearer than the near.

HE.

Distance is nearer than proximity,
When distance longs, proximity doth not.

SHE.

The near is always distant to the mind
That craves for satisfaction of its end ;

Nor doth the distance ever feel so far
As when the end is touched.　Retard that goal,
Prolonging appetite beyond the feast
That feeds anticipation.

HE.

　　　　　Specious foil!
That parries every stroke before 'tis made.
Yet surfeit's self doth not more surely cloy
Than endless fasting.

SHE.

　　　　　Still a swifter cure
Waits on too little than attends too much.
While disappointment merely woundeth Hope,
The deadly blow by disenchantment dealt
Strikes at the heart of Faith.　O happy you,
The favourites of Fancy, who replace
Illusion with illusion, and conceive
Fresh cradles in the dark womb of the grave.
While we, prosaic victims, prove that time
Kills love while leaving loveless life alive,
You still, divinely duped, sing deathless love,
And with your wizard music, once again,

E

Make Winter Spring.   Yet surely you forgive
That I have too much pity for the flowers
Children and poets cull to fling away,
To be an April nosegay.

HE.

How you swell
The common chorus !   Women, who are wronged
So roughly by men's undiscerning word,
As though one pattern served to show them all,
Should be more just to poets.   These, in truth,
Diverge from one another nowise less
Than " women," vaguely labelled : children some,
With childish voice and nature, lyric bards,
Weaklings that on life's threshold sweetly wail,
But never from that silvery treble pass
Into the note and chant of manliness.
Their love is like their verse, a frail desire,
A fluttering fountain falling feebly back
Into its shallow origin.   Next there are
The poets of contention, wrestlers born,
Who challenge iron Circumstance, and fail :
Generous and strong, withal not strong enough,
Since lacking sinewy wisdom, hard as life.

The love of these is like the lightning spear,
And shrivels whom it touches.   They consume
All things within their reach, and, last of all,
Their lonely selves ; and then through time they tower,
Sublime but charred, and wear on their high fronts
The gloomy glory of the sunlit pine.
But the great gods of Song, in clear white light,
The radiance of their godhead, calmly dwell,
And with immutable cold starlike gaze
Scan both the upper and the under world,
As it revolves, themselves serenely fixed.
Their bias is the bias of the sphere,
That turns all ways, but turns away from none,
Save to return to it.   They have no feud
With gods or men, the living or the dead,
The past or present, and their words complete
Life's incompleteness with a healing note.
For they are not more sensitive than strong,
More wise than tender ; understanding all,
At peace with all, at peace with life and death,
And love that gives a meaning unto life
And takes from death the meaning and the sting :
At peace with hate, and every opposite.
Were I but one of these—presumptuous thought !—

Even you, the live fulfilment of such dreams
As these secrete, would hazard well your love
On my more largely loving.　'Twould be you,
Yes, even you, that first would flag and fail
In either of my choosing; you, whose wing
Would droop on mine and pray to be upborne.
And when my pinions did no more suffice
For that their double load, then softly down,
Softly and smoothly as descending lark
That hath fulfilled its rhapsody in Heaven,
And with diminished music must decline
To earthy sounds and concepts, I should curb
Illimitable longings to the range
Of lower aspiration.　Were I such !—
But, since I *am* not—

SHE.

　　　　　　Am not ?　Who shall say,
Save she who tests, and haply to her loss?
'Tis better left untested.　Strange that you,
Who can imagine whatso thing you will,
Should lack imagination to appraise
Imagination at its topmost worth.
Now wield your native sceptre and extend

Your fancy forth where Florence overbrims
In eddies fairer even than herself.
Look how the landscape smiles complacently
At its own beauty, as indeed it may;
Villa and vineyard each a separate home,
Containing possibilities unseen,
Materials for your pleasure.   Now disport!
Which homestead may it please my lord of song
To chalk for his, as those rough Frenchmen did
Who came with bow-legged Charles to justify
Savonarola's scourgeful prophecies?
Shall it be that one gazing in our face,
Not jealous of its beauty, but exposed
To all the wantonness of sun and air,
With roses girt, with roses garlanded,
And balustraded terrace topped with jars
Of clove carnations; unambitious roof,
Italian equivalent to house
Love in a cottage?   Why, the very place
For her you once described!   Wait!   Let me see,
Can I recall the lines?   Yes, thus they ran.
Do you remember them?   Or are they now
A chronicle forgotten and erased
From that convenient palimpsest, the heart?

In dewy covert of her eyes
The secret of the violet lies ;
The sun and wind caress and pair
In the lithe wavelets of her hair ;
The fragrance of the warm soft south
Hovers about her honeyed mouth ;
And, when she moves, she floats through air
Like zephyr-wafted gossamer.
Hers is no lore of dumb dead books ;
Her learning liveth in her looks ;
And still she shows, in meek replies,
Wisdom enough to deem you wise.
Her voice as soothing is and sweet
As whispers of the waving wheat,
And in the moisture of her kiss
Is April-like deliciousness.
Like gloaming-hour, she doth inspire
A vague, an infinite desire ;
And, like the stars, though out of sight,
Filleth the loneliness of night.
Come how she may, or slow or fleet.
She brings the morning on her feet ;
Gone, leaves behind a nameless pain,
Like the sadness of a silenced strain.

HE.

A youthful dream.

SHE.

    Yet memory can surmise
That young dream fruited to reality,
Then, like reality, was dream no more.
All dreams are youthful ; you are dreaming still.
What lovely visions denizen your sleep !
Let me recall another ; for I know
All you have written, thought, and felt, and much
You neither thought nor felt, but only sang.
A wondrous gift, a godlike gift, that breathes
Into our exiled clay unexiled lives,
Manlier than Adam, comelier than Eve.
That massive villa, we both know so well,
With one face set toward Settignano, one
Gazing at Bellosguardo, and its rear
Locked from the north by clustered cypresses,
That seem like fixed colossal sentinels,
And tower above its tower, but look not in,
Might be abode for her whom you conceived
In tropes so mystical, you must forgive
If recollection trips.

To dwell with her is calmly to abide
Through every change of time and every flux of tide.

In her the Present, Past, and Future meet,
The Father, and the Son, and dovelike Paraclete.

She holdeth silent intercourse with Night,
Still journeying with the stars, and shining with their
*   light.*

Her love, illumination ; her embrace,
The sweep of angels' wings across a mortal's face.

Her lap is piled with autumn fruits, her brow
Crowned with the blossoming trails that smile from
*   April's bough.*

Like wintry stars that shine with frosty fire,
Her loftiness excites to elevate desire.

To love her is to burn with such a flame
As lights the lamp which bears the Sanctuary's name.

That lamp burns on for ever, day and night,
Before her mystic shrine.   I am its acolyte.

HE.

The merest foam of fancy ; foam and spray.

SHE.

Foam-drift of fancy that hath ebbed away.
See how the very simile rebukes
Man's all unsealike longings!   For confess,
While ocean still returns, the puny waves
Of mortal love are sucked into the sand,
Their motion felt, their music heard, no more.
Look when the vines are linking hands, and seem
As pausing from the dance of Spring, or just
Preparing to renew it, round and round,
On the green carpet of the bladed corn,
That spreads about their feet : corn, vine, and fig,
Almond and mulberry, cherry, and pear, and peach,
Not taught to know their place, but left to range
Up to the villa's walls, windows, and doors,
And peep into its life and smile good-day,
A portion of its homeliness and joy :
A poet's villa once, a poet's again,
If you but dream it such ; a roof for her,

To whom you wrote—I wonder who she was—
This saucy sonnet; saucy, withal sweet,
And O, how true of the reflected love
You poets render to your worshippers.

TRUE AS THE DIAL TO THE SUN.

You are the sun, and I the dial, sweet,
So you can mark on me what time you will.
If you move slowly, how can I move fleet?
And when you halt, I too must fain be still.
Chide not the cloudy humours of my brow,
If you behold no settled sunshine there:
Rather upbraid your own, sweet, and allow,
My looks cannot be foul if yours be fair.
Then from the heaven of your high witchery shine,
And I with smiles shall watch the hours glide by;
You have no mood that is not straightway mine;
My cheek but takes complexion from your eye.
All that I am dependeth so on you,
What clouds the sun must cloud the dial too.

HE.

No man should quarrel with his Past, and I
Maintain no feud with mine.   Do we not ripen,
Ripen and mellow in love, unto the close,
Thanks no more to the present than the past?
First love is fresh but fugitive as Spring,
A wilding flower no sooner plucked than faded;
And summer's sultry fervour ends in storm,
Recriminating thunder, wasteful tears,
And angry gleam of lightning menaces.
Give me October's meditative haze,
Its gossamer mornings, dewy-wimpled eves,
Dewy and fragrant, fragrant and secure,
. The long slow sound of farmward-wending wains,
When homely Love sups quiet 'mong its sheaves,
Sups 'mong its sheaves, its sickle at its side,
And all is peace, peace and plump fruitfulness.

SHE.

Picture of all we dream and we desire:
Autumn's grave cheerfulness and sober bliss,
Rich resignation, humble constancy.
For, prone to bear the load piled up by life,

We, once youth's pasture season at an end,
Submit to crawl.   Unbroken to the last,
You spurn the goad of stern taskmaster Time.
Even 'mid autumn harvest you demand
Returning hope and blossom of the Spring,
All seasons and sensations, and at once,
Or in too quick succession.   Do we blame?
We envy rather the eternal youth
We cannot share.   But youth is pitiless,
And, marching onward, neither asks nor seeks
Who falls behind.   Thus women who are wise,
Beside their thresholds knitting homely gear,
Wave wistful salutation as you pass,
And think of you regretfully, when gone :
A soft regret, a sweet regret, that is
Only the mellow fruit of unplucked joy.
Now improvise some other simple strain,
That with harmonious cadence may attune
The vain and hazard discords of discourse.

HE.

When Love was young, it asked for wings,
That it might still be roaming ;

And away it sped, by fancy led,
   Through dawn, and noon, and gloaming.
Each daintiness that blooms and blows
   It wooed in honeyed metre,
And when it won the sweetest sweet,
   It flew off to a sweeter :
      When Love was young.

When Love was old, it craved for rest,
   For home, and hearth, and haven ;
For quiet talks round sheltered walks,
   And long lawns smoothly shaven.
And what Love sought, at last it found,
   A roof, a porch, a garden,
And from a fond unquestioning heart
   Peace, sympathy, and pardon,
      When Love was old.

SHE.

Simple, in sooth, and haply true : withal,
Too, too autumnal even for my heart.
I never weary of your vernal note.
Carol again, and sing me back my youth
With the redundant melodies of Spring.

HE.

I breathe my heart in the heart of the rose,
  The rose that I pluck and send you,
With a prayer that the perfume its leaves enclose
  May kiss, and caress, and tend you:
Caress and tend you till I can come,
  To the garden where first I found you,
And the thought that as yet in the rose is dumb
  Can ripple in music round you.

O rose, that will shortly be her guest,
  You may well look happy, at leaving:
Will you lie in the cradle her snowy breast
  Doth rock with its gentle heaving?
Will you mount the throne of her hazel hair,
  That waves like a summer billow,
Or be hidden and hushed, at nightfall prayer,
  In the folds of her dimpled pillow?

And when she awakes at dawn to feel
  If you have been dreaming with her,
Then the whole of your secret, sweet rose, reveal,
  And say I am coming thither:

And that when there is silence in earth and sky,
  And peace from the cares that cumber,
She must not ask if your leaves or I
  Be clasped in her perfumed slumber.

SHE.

Give me your hand ; and, if you will, keep mine
Engraffed in yours, as slowly thus we skirt
La Doccia's dark declivity, and make
Athwart Majano's pathless pines a path
To lead us onward haply where it may.
Lo ! the Carrara mountains flush to view,
That in the noonday were not visible.
Shall we not fold this comfort to our hearts,
Humbly rejoiced to think as there are heights
Seen only in the sunset, so our lives,
If that they lack not loftiness, may wear
A glow of glory on their furrowed fronts,
Until they faint and fade into the night !

AN APRIL LOVE

NAY, be not June, nor yet December, dear,
But April always, as I find thee now:
A constant freshness unto me be thou,
And not the ripeness that must soon be sere.
Why should I be Time's dupe, and wish more near
The sobering harvest of thy vernal vow?
I am content, so still across thy brow
Returning smile chase transitory tear.
Then scatter thy April heart in sunny showers;
I want nor Summer drouth nor Winter sleet:
As Spring be fickle, so thou be as sweet;
With half-kept promise tantalise the hours;
And let Love's frolic hands and woodland feet
Fill high the lap of Life with wilding flowers.

WHEN ACORNS FALL

WHEN acorns fall and swallows troop for flight,
And hope matured slow mellows to regret,
And Autumn, pressed by Winter for his debt,
Drops leaf on leaf till she be beggared quite ;
Should then the crescent moon's unselfish light
Gleam up the sky, just as the sun doth set,
Her brightening gaze, though day and dark have met,
Prolongs the gloaming and retards the night.
So, fair young life, new risen upon mine
Just as it owns the edict of decay
And Fancy's fires should pale and pass away,
My menaced glory takes a glow from thine,
And, in the deepening sundown of my day,
Thou with thy dawn delayest my decline.

F

IN THE HEART OF THE FOREST

I

I HEARD the voice of my own true love
    Ripple the sunny weather.
Then away, as a dove that follows a dove,
    We flitted through woods together.

II

There was not a bush nor branch nor spray
    But with song was swaying and ringing.
" Let us ask of the birds what means their lay,
    And what is it prompts their singing."

III

We paused where the stichwort and speedwell grew
    Mid a forest of grasses fairy :
From out of the covert the cushat flew,
    And the squirrel perched shy and wary.

IV

On an elm-tree top shrilled a misselthrush proud,
  Disdaining shelter or screening.
" Now what is it makes you pipe so loud,
  And what is your music's meaning ?

V

" Your matins begin ere the dewdrop sinks
  To the heart of the moist musk-roses,
And your vespers last till the first star winks,
  And the vigilant woodreeve dozes."

VI

Then louder, still louder he shrilled : " I sing
  For the pleasure and pride of shrilling,
For the sheen and the sap and the showers of Spring
  That fill me to overfilling.

VII

" Yet a something deeper than Spring-time, though
  It is Spring-like, my throat keeps flooding :
Peep soft at my mate,—she is there below,—
  Where the bramble trails are budding.

VIII

" She sits on the nest and she never stirs ;
   She is true to the trust I gave her ;
And what were my love if I cheered not hers
   As long as my throat can quaver ? "

IX

So he quavered on, till asudden we heard
   A voice that called " Cuckoo ! " and fleeted.
" Why all day is your name by yourself, vain bird,
   Repeated and still repeated ? "

X

Then " Cuckoo ! Cuck ! Cuck ! Cuck-oo ! " he called,
   And he laughed and he chuckled cheerly ;
" Your hearts they run dry and your heads grow bald,
   But I come back with April yearly.

XI

" I come in the month that is sweet, so sweet,
   Though its sweetness be frail and fickle,
In the season when shower and sunshine meet,
   And you reck not of Autumn's sickle.

XII

" I flout at the April loves of men
  And the kisses of shy fond maidens ;
And then I call ' Cuckoo !' again, again,
  With a jeering and jocund cadence.

XIII

" When the hawthorn blows and the yaffel mates,
  I sing and am silent never ;
Just as love of itself in the May-time prates,
  As though it will last for ever !

XIV

" And in June, ere I go, I double the note,
  As I flit from cover to cover :
Are not vows, at the last, repeated by rote
  By fading and fleeting lover ?"

XV

A tear trickled down my true love's cheek
  At the words of the mocking rover ;
She clung to my side, but she did not speak,
  And I kissed her over and over.

XVI

And while she leaned on my heart as though
  Her love in its depths was rooting,
There rose from the thicket behind us, slow,
  O such a silvery fluting!

XVII

When the long smooth note, as it seemed, must break,
  It fell in a swift sweet treble,
Like the sound that is made when a stream from a lake
  Gurgles o'er stone and pebble.

XVIII

And I cried, "O nightingale! tell me true,
  Is your music rapture or weeping?
And why do you sing the whole night through,
  When the rest of the world is sleeping?"

XIX

Then it fluted: "My notes are of love's pure strain,
  And could there be descant fitter?
For why do you sever joy and pain,
  Since love is both sweet and bitter?

XX

" My song now wails of the sighs, the tears,
  The long absence that makes love languish;
Then thrills with its fluttering hopes and fears,
  Its rapture,—again its anguish.

XXI

" And why should my notes be hushed at night?
  Why sing in the sunlight only?
Love loves when 'tis dark, as when 'tis bright,
  Nor ceaseth because 'tis lonely."

XXII

My love looked up with a happy smile,
  (For a moment the woods were soundless):
The smile of a heart that knows no guile,
  And whose trust is deep and boundless.

XXIII

And as I smiled that her smile betrayed
  The fulness of love's surrender,
Came a note from the heart of the forest shade,
  O so soft, and smooth, and tender!

XXIV

'Twas but one note, and it seemed to brood
  On its own sufficing sweetness ;
That cooed, and cooed, and again but cooed
  In a round, self-same completeness.

XXV

Then I said, " There is, ringdove, endless bliss
  In the sound that you keep renewing :
But have you no other note than this,
  And why are you always cooing?"

XXVI

The ringdove answered : " I too descant
  Of love as the woods keep closing ;
Not of spring-time loves that exult and pant,
  But of harvest love reposing.

XXVII

" If I coo all day on the self-same bough,
  While the noisy popinjay ranges,
'Tis that love which is mellow keeps its vow,
  And callow love shifts and changes.

XXVIII

" When summer shall silence the merle's loud throat
  And the nightingale's sweet sad singing,
You still will hear my contented note,
  On the branch where I now am clinging.

XXIX

" For the rapture of fancy surely wanes,
  And anguish is lulled by reason ;
But the tender note of the heart remains
  Through all changes of leaf and season."

XXX

Then we plunged in the forest, my love and I,
  In the forest plunged deeper and deeper,
Till none could behold us save only the sky,
  Through a trellis of branch and creeper.

XXXI

And we paired and nested away from sight
  In a bower of woodbine pearly ;
And she broods on our love from morn to night,
  And I sing to her late and early.

XXXII

Nor till Death shall have stripped our lives as bare
  As the forest in wintry weather,
Will the world find the nest in the covert where
  We dwelt, loved, and sang together.

WHY ENGLAND IS CONSERVATIVE

I

BECAUSE of our dear Mother, the fair Past,
On whom twin Hope and Memory safely lean,
And from whose fostering wisdom none shall wean
Their love and faith, while love and faith shall last :
Mother of happy homes and Empire vast,
Of hamlet snug, and many a proud demesne,
Blue spires of cottage smoke 'mong woodlands green,
And comely altars where no stone is cast.
And shall we barter these for gaping Throne,
Dismantled towers, mean plots without a tree,
A herd of hinds too equal to be free,
Greedy of other's, jealous of their own,
And, where sweet Order now breathes cadenced tone,
Envy, and hate, and all uncharity ?

II

Banish the fear!   'Twere infamy to yield
To folly what to force had been denied,
Or in the Senate quail before the tide
We should have stemmed and routed in the field.
What though no more we brandish sword and shield,
Reason's keen blade is ready at our side,
And manly brains, in wisdom panoplied,
Can foil the shafts that treacherous sophists wield.
The spirit of our fathers is not quelled.
With weapons valid even as those they bore,
Domain, Throne, Altar, still may be upheld,
So we disdain, as they disdained of yore,
The foreign froth that foams against our shore,
Only by its white cliffs to be repelled!

III

Therefore, chime sweet and safely, village bells,
And, rustic chancels, woo to reverent prayer,
And, wise and simple, to the porch repair
Round which Death, slumbering, dreamlike heaves
   and swells.
Let hound and horn in wintry woods and dells
Make jocund music though the boughs be bare,
And whistling yokel guide his gleaming share
Hard by the homes where gentle lordship dwells.
Therefore sit high enthroned on every hill,
Authority ! and loved in every vale ;
Nor, old Tradition, falter in the tale
Of lowly valour led by lofty will :
And, though the throats of envy rage and rail,
Be fair proud England proud fair England still !

THE OWL AND THE LARK

I

A GRIZZLED owl at midnight moped
   Where thick the ivy glistened;
So I, who long have vainly groped
   For wisdom, leaned and listened.

II

Its perch was firm, its aspect staid,
   Its big eyes gleamed and brightened;
Now, now at last, will doubt be laid,
   Now yearning be enlightened.

III

" Tu-whit! Tu-whoo!" the bird discoursed,
   " Tu-whoo! Tu-whit!" repeated:
Showing how matter was, when forced
   Through space, condensed and heated;

IV

How rent, but spinning still, 'twas sphered
  In star, and orb, and planet,
Where, as it cooled, live germs appeared
  In lias, sand, and granite :

V

And, last, since nothing 'neath the sun
  Avoids material tether,
How life must end, when once begun,
  In scale, and hoof, and feather.

VI

Then, flapping from the ivy-tod,
  It slouched around the gable,
And, perching there, discussed if God
  Be God, or but a fable.

VII

In pompous scales Free Will and Fate
  Were placed, and poised, and dangled,
And riddles small from riddles great
  Expertly disentangled.

VIII

It drew betwixt " Tu-whit," " Tu-whoo,"
    Distinctions nice and nicer :
The bird was very wise, I knew,
    But I grew no whit wiser.

IX

Then, letting metaphysics slip,
    It mumbled moral thunder ;
Showing how Virtue's self will trip
    If Reason chance to blunder.

X

Its pleated wings adown its breast
    Were like a surplice folded ;
And, if the truth must be confessed,
    It threatened me and scolded.

XI

I thought the lecture somewhat long,
    Impatient for its ending ;
When, sudden, came a burst of song !
    It was the lark ascending.

XII

Dew gleamed in many a jewelled cup,
  The air was bright and gracious ;
And away the wings and the song went up,
  Up through the ether spacious.

XIII

They bubbled, rippled, up the dome,
  In sprays of silvery trilling ;
Like endless fountain's lyric foam,
  Still falling, still refilling.

XIV

And when I could no more descry
  The bird, I still could hear it ;
For sight, but not for soul, too high,
  Unseen but certain Spirit.

XV

All that the perched owl's puckered brow
  Had vainly bid me ponder,
The lark's light wings were solving now
  In the roofless dome up yonder.

G

XVI

Then brief as lightning-flash,—no more,—
   I passed beyond the Finite;
And, borne past Heaven's wide-open door,
   Saw everything within it.

XVII

Slow showering down from cloudless sphere,
   The wanderer Elysian
Dropped nearer, clearer, to the ear,
   Then back into the vision.

XVIII

On his own song he seemed to swim;
   Diving through song, descended:
Since I had been to Heaven with him,
   Earth now was apprehended.

XIX

O souls perplexed by hood and cowl,
   Fain would you find a teacher,
Consult the lark and not the owl,
   The poet, not the preacher.

xx

While brains mechanic vainly weave
   The web and woof of thinking,
Go, mount up with the lark, and leave
   The bird of wisdom blinking.

A MEETING

NOVEMBER 19, 1888

QUEEN, widowed Mother of a widowed child,
Whose ancient sorrow goeth forth to meet
Her new-born sorrow with parental feet,
And tearful eyes that oft on hers have smiled,
Will not your generous heart be now beguiled
From its too lonely anguish, as You greet
Her anguish, yet more cruel and complete,
And, through her woe, with woe be reconciled?
Or if this may not be, and all the years
Of love's bereavement be withal too brief
To bring slow solace to still lengthening grief
For loss of One whom distance but endears,
Surely to Both will come some sad relief,
Sharing the comfort of commingled tears.

STAFFORD HENRY NORTHCOTE

GENTLE in fibre, but of steadfast nerve
Still to do right though right won blame not praise,
And fallen on evil tongues and evil days [1]
When men from plain straight duty twist and swerve,
And, born to nobly sway, ignobly serve,
Sliming their track to power through tortuous ways,
He felt, with that fine sense that ne'er betrays,
The line of moral beauty 's not a curve.
But, proving wisdom folly, virtue vain,
He stretched his hands out to the other shore, [2]
And was by kindred spirits beckoned o'er
Into the gloaming Land where setteth pain,
While we across the silent river strain
Idly our gaze, and find his form no more.

[1] ". . . Though fallen on evil days,
On evil days though fallen, and evil tongues."
Paradise Lost, Book VII. v. 25, 26.
[2] "Tendebantque manus ripæ ulterioris amore."
Æneidos Lib. VI. v. 314.

IN THE MONTH WHEN SINGS
THE CUCKOO

I

HARK ! Spring is coming. Her herald sings,
                              Cuckoo !
The air resounds and the woodland rings,
                              Cuckoo ! Cuckoo !
Leave the milking pail and the mantling cream,
And down by the meadow, and up by the stream,
Where movement is music and life a dream,
              In the month when sings the cuckoo.

II

Away with old Winter's frowns and fears,
                              Cuckoo ! Cuckoo !
Now May with a smile dries April's tears.
                              Cuckoo !

When the bees are humming in bloom and bud,
And the kine sit chewing the moist green cud,
Shall the snow not melt in a maiden's blood,
  In the month when sings the cuckoo?

III

The popinjay mates and the lapwing woos;
    Cuckoo!
In the lane is a footstep. I wonder whose?
    Cuckoo! Cuckoo!
How sweet are low whispers! and sweet, so sweet,
When the warm hands touch and the shy lips meet,
And sorrel and woodruff are round our feet,
  In the month when sings the cuckoo.

IV

Your face is as fragrant as moist musk-rose;
    Cuckoo! Cuckoo!
All the year in your cheek the windflower blows;
    Cuckoo! Cuckoo!
You flit as blithely as bird on wing;

And when you answer, and when they sing,
I know not if they, or You, be Spring,
   In the month when pairs the cuckoo.

V

Will you love me still when the blossom droops?
        Cuckoo !
When the cracked husk falls and the fieldfare troops?
        Cuckoo !
Let sere leaf or snowdrift shade your brow,
By the soul of the Spring, sweet-heart, I vow,
I will love you then as I love you now,
   In the month when sings the cuckoo.

VI

Smooth, smooth is the sward where the loosestrife grows,
      Cuckoo ! Cuckoo !
As we lie and hear in a dreamy doze,
     Cuckoo ! Cuckoo ! Cuckoo !
And smooth is the curve of a maiden's cheek,
When she loves to listen but fears to speak,

And we yearn but we know not what we seek,
    In the month when sings the cuckoo.

VII

But in warm mid summer we hear no more,
                Cuckoo !
And August brings not, with all its store,
                Cuckoo !
When Autumn shivers on Winter's brink,
And the wet wind wails through crevice and chink,
We gaze at the logs, and sadly think
    Of the month when called the cuckoo.

VIII

But the cuckoo comes back and shouts once more,
                Cuckoo !
And the world is as young as it was before :
              Cuckoo ! Cuckoo !
It grows not older for mortal tears,
For the falsehood of men or for women's fears ;
'Tis as young as it was in the bygone years,
    When first was heard the cuckoo.

IX

I will love you then as I love you now.

            Cuckoo!

What cares the Spring for a broken vow?

            Cuckoo! Cuckoo!

The broods of last year are pairing, this;

And there never will lack, while love is bliss,

Fresh ears to cozen, fresh lips to kiss,

        In the month when sings the cuckoo.

X

O cruel bird! will you never have done?

         Cuckoo! Cuckoo! Cuckoo!

You sing for the cloud, as you sang for the sun;

          Cuckoo! Cuckoo!

You mock me now as you mocked me then,

When I knew not yet that the loves of men

Are as brief as the glamour of glade and glen,

       And the glee of the fleeting cuckoo.

XI

O, to lie once more in the long fresh grass,

            Cuckoo!

And dream of the sounds and scents that pass ;

                Cuckoo ! Cuckoo !

To savour the woodbine, surmise the dove,

With no roof save the far-off sky above,

And a curtain of kisses round couch of love,

      While distantly called the cuckoo.

XII

But if now I slept, I should sleep to wake

To the sleepless pang and the dreamless ache,

To the wild babe blossom within my heart,

To the darkening terror and swelling smart,

To the searching look and the words apart,

      And the hint of the tell-tale cuckoo.

XIII

The meadow grows thick, and the stream runs deep,

                  Cuckoo !

Where the aspens quake and the willows weep ;

             Cuckoo ! Cuckoo !

The dew of the night and the morning heat

Will close up the track of my farewell feet :—·
So good-bye to the life that once was sweet,
  When so sweetly called the cuckoo.

XIV

The kine are unmilked, and the cream unchurned,
    Cuckoo!
The pillow unpressed, and the quilt unturned,
    Cuckoo! Cuckoo!
'Twas easy to gibe at a beldame's fear
For the quick brief blush and the sidelong tear;
But if maids will gad in the youth of the year,
  They should heed what says the cuckoo.

XV

There are marks in the meadow laid up for hay,
    Cuckoo!
And the tread of a foot where no foot should stray :
    Cuckoo! Cuckoo!
The banks of the pool are broken down,
Where the water is quiet and deep and brown ;—
The very spot, if one longed to drown,
  And no more to hear the cuckoo.

XVI

'Tis a full taut net and a heavy haul.

Cuckoo! Cuckoo!

Look! her auburn hair and her trim new shawl!

Cuckoo! Cuckoo!

Draw a bit this way where 'tis not so steep;

There, cover her face! She but seems asleep;

While the swallows skim and the graylings leap,

And joyously sings the cuckoo.

THE DREGS OF LOVE

THINK you that I will drain the dregs of Love,
I who have quaffed the sweetness on its brink?
Now by the steadfast burning stars above,
Better to faint of thirst than thuswise drink.
What! shall we twain who saw love's glorious fires
Flame toward the sky and flush Heaven's self with
     light,
Crouch by the embers as the glow expires,
And huddle closer from mere dread of night?
No! cast love's goblet in oblivion's well,
Scatter love's ashes o'er the field of time!
Yet, ere we part, one kiss whereon to dwell
When life sounds senseless as some feeble rhyme.
Lo! as lips touch, anew Love's cresset glows,
And Love's sweet cup refills and overflows.

A FAREWELL TO YOUTH

Ere that I say farewell to youth, and take
The homely road that leads to life's decline,
Let me be sure again I shall not pine
To taste the bliss you bid me to forsake :
That Spring's returning raptures will not wake
Too late repentance for abjuring mine,
Nor the old sweets I pledge me to resign
Behind them leave the bitterness of ache.
Yet is there nothing of one's generous prime
To bear me kindred company to the end,
Some passionate longing, some belief sublime,
Some wrong to right, some failure to befriend?
Leave me but these, I care not where I wend,
But down life's slope go hand-in-hand with Time. ·

A MARCH MINSTREL

I

HAIL! once again, that sweet strong note!
    Loud on my loftiest larch,
Thou quaverest with thy mottled throat,
    Brave minstrel of bleak March!

II

Hearing thee flute, who pines or grieves
    For vernal smiles and showers?
Thy voice is greener than the leaves,
    And fresher than the flowers.

III

Scorning to wait for tuneful May
    When every throat can sing,
Thou floutest Winter with thy lay,
    And art thyself the Spring!

IV

While daffodils, half mournful still,
　　Muffle their golden bells,
Thy silvery peal o'er landscape chill
　　Surges, and sinks, and swells.

V

Across the unsheltered pasture floats
　　The young lamb's shivering bleat.
There is no trembling in thy notes,
　　For all the snow and sleet.

VI

Let the bullace bide till frosts have ceased,
　　The blackthorn loiter long;
Undaunted by the blustering east,
　　Thou burgeonest into song.

VII

Yet who can wonder thou dost dare
　　Confront what others flee?
Thy carol cuts the keen March air
　　Keener than it cuts Thee.

H

VIII

The selfish cuckoo tarrieth till
  April repays his boast.
Thou, thou art lavish of thy trill,
  Now when we need it most.

IX

The nightingale, while buds are coy,
  Delays to chant its grief.
Brave throstle ! thou dost pipe for joy,
  With never a bough in leaf.

X

Even fond turtle-doves forbear
  To coo till woods are warm :
Thou hast the heart to love and pair
  Ere the cherry blossoms swarm.

XI

The skylark, fluttering to be heard
  In realms beyond his birth,
Soars vainly heavenward.   Thou, wise bird !
  Art satisfied with earth.

XII

Thy home is not upon the ground,
  Thy hope not in the sky :
Near to thy nest thy notes resound,
  Neither too low nor high.

XIII

Blow what wind will, thou dost rejoice
  To carol, and build, and woo.
Throstle ! to me impart thy voice ;
  Impart thy wisdom too.

LOVE'S UNITY

How can I tell thee when I love thee best?
In rapture or repose? how shall I say?
I only know I love thee every way,
Plumed for love's flight, or folded in love's nest.
See, what is day but night bedewed with rest?
And what the night except the tired-out day?
And 'tis love's difference, not love's decay,
If now I dawn, now fade, upon thy breast.
Self-torturing sweet!   Is't not the self-same sun
Wanes in the west that flameth in the east,
His fervour nowise altered nor decreased?
So rounds my love, returning where begun,
And still beginning, never most nor least,
But fixedly various, all love's parts in one.

TWO VISIONS

WRITTEN, 1863.   REVISED, 1889

I

THE curtains of the night were folded
  Round sleep-entangled sense ;
So that the things I saw were moulded,
  I know not how, nor whence.

II

But I beheld a smokeless city,
  Built upon jutting slopes,
Up whose steep paths, as if for pity,
  Stretched loosely-hanging ropes.

III

Withal, of many who ascended,
  No one appeared to use
This aid, allowed in days since mended,
  When folks had weaker thews.

IV

The men, still animal in vigour,
  Strode stalwart and erect;
But on their brows, in placid rigour,
  Reigned sovereign Intellect.

V

Women round-limbed, sound-lunged, full-
    breasted,
  Walked at a rhythmic pace;
Yet not the less, for that, invested
  With every female grace.

VI

Fearless, unveiled, and unattended,
  Strolled maidens to and fro:
Youths looked respect, but never bended
  Obsequiously low.

VII

And each with other, sans condition,
  Held parley brief or long,
Without provoking coarse suspicion
  Of marriage, or of wrong.

VIII

All were well clad, but none were better,
    And gems beheld I none,
Save where there hung a jewelled fetter,
    Symbolic, in the sun.

IX

I saw a noble-looking maiden
    Close Dante's solemn book,
And go, with crate of linen laden,
    And wash it in the brook.

X

Anon, a broad-browed poet, dragging
    A load of logs along,
To warm his hearth, withal not flagging
    In current of his song.

XI

Each one some handicraft attempted,
    Or helped to till the soil :
None but the agëd were exempted
    From communistic toil :

XII

Which was nor long nor unremitting,
  Since shared in by the whole ;
Leaving to each one, as is fitting,
  Full leisure for the Soul.

XIII

Was many a group in allocution
  On problems that delight,
And lift, when e'en beyond solution,
  Man to a nobler height.

XIV

And oftentimes was brave contention,
  Such as beseems the wise ;
But always courteous abstention
  From over-swift replies

XV

Age lorded not, nor rose the hectic
  Up to the cheek of Youth ;
But reigned throughout their dialectic
  Sobriety of truth.

XVI

And if a long-held contest tended
　To ill-defined result,
It was by calm consent suspended
　As over-difficult :

XVII

And verse or music was suggested,
　Then solitude of night :
Whereby the senses are invested
　With spiritual sight.

XVIII

So far, the city.　All around it
　Olive, or vine, or corn ;
Those having pressed, or trod, or ground it,
　By these 'twas townward borne,

XIX

And placed in halls unbarred though splendid,
　With none to overlook,
And whither each at leisure wended,
　And, what he wanted, took.

XX

And men saluted one the other,
　Or as they passed or stood,
" Let us still love and labour, brother,
　For life is sweet and good."

XXI

I saw no crippled forms nor meagre,
　None smitten by disease :
Only the old, nor loth nor eager,
　Dying by kind degrees.

XXII

And when, without or pain or trouble,
　They sank as sinks the sun,
" This is the sole Inevitable,"
　All said ; " His will be done !"

XXIII

And went, with music softly swelling,
　Where land o'erlooks the sea,
Over the corse piled herbs sweet-smelling,
　Consumed, and so set free.

XXIV

Past ocean wave and mountain daisy
  As curled the perfumed smoke,
The notes grew faint, the vision hazy :—
  Straining my sense, I woke.

    *   *   *   *   *

XXV

SWIFT I arose. Soft winds were stirring
  The curtains of the Morn,
Promise of day, by signs unerring,
  Lovely as e'er was born.

XXVI

But here the pleasant likeness ended
  Between the cities twain :
Level and straight these streets extended
  Over an easy plain.

XXVII

Withal, the people who thus early
  Began to troop and throng,
With curving back and visage surly
  Toiled painfully along.

XXVIII

Groups of them met at yet closed portals,
  And huddled round the gate,
Patient, as smit by the Immortals,
  And helots as by Fate.

XXIX

Full many a cross-crowned front and steeple
  Clave the cerulean air :
As grew the concourse of the people,
  They rang to rival prayer.

XXX

On their confronting walls were posted
  Placards in glaring type,
Whereof there was not one but boasted
  Truth full-grown, round, and ripe.

XXXI

And, with this self-congratulation,
  Each one the other banned,
With threats of durable damnation
  From the Eternal Hand.

XXXII

Surmounting these, were Forms forbidding
  Disputes about the Flood ;
Since, in such points divine unthridding,
  Shed had been human blood.

XXXIII

From arch and alley sodden wretches
  Crept out in half attire,
And groped for fetid husks and vetches
  In heaps of tossed-out mire ;

XXXIV

Until disturbed by horses' trample,
  And faces fair and gay,
Which, sleek and warm, with ermines ample,
  And glittering diamond spray

XXXV

That lightly flecked the classic ripple
  Of their flower-scented hair,
For shivering child and leprous cripple
  Had not a look to spare.

XXXVI

In garments with the morn ill mated,
  Anon came youths along ;
From side to side they oscillated,
  And trolled a shameful song.

XXXVII

Thereat my heart, this longwhile throbbing,
  With teardrops sought to ease
O'erwelling woe, and wildly sobbing,
  I fell upon my knees.

XXXVIII

And made irreverent by the fluster
  Of sorrow's fierce extreme,
I cried, "O unjust Heaven ! be juster,
  And realise my dream !"

XXXIX

Up streamed the sun, and straight were shining
  Steeple, and sill, and roof:
To my hot prayer and rash repining
  A visible reproof.

XL

Rebuked, I rose from genuflexion,
   And, ceasing to blaspheme,
Curtained mine eyes for introspection
   Of the departed dream,

XLI

Where men saluted one the other,
   In street, or field, or wood,
"Let us still love and labour, brother;
   For life is sweet and good."

XLII

And I resolved, by contrast smitten,
   To live and strive by Law;
And first to write, as here are written,
   The Visions Twain I saw.

NOCTURNAL VIGILS

WHY do you chide me that, when mortals yield
To slumber's charm, from sleep I ask no boon,
But from my casement watch the maimëd moon
Fainting behind her ineffectual shield:
Unto the chime by stately planets pealed
My song, my soul, my very self attune,
And nightly see, what none can see at noon,
The runic volume of the sky unsealed?
Haply the hour may come when grateful Night
Will these brief vigils endlessly repay,
And, on the dwindling of my earthly day,
Keep, like her stars, my heavenly fancies bright;
And glorious dreamings, shrouded now from sight,
Dawn out of darkness, not to sleep for aye.

TO LORD TENNYSON

POET ! in other lands, when Spring no more
Gleams o'er the grass, nor in the thicket-side
Plays at being lost and laughs to be descried,
And blooms lie wilted on the orchard floor,
Then the sweet birds that from Ægean shore
Across Ausonian breakers hither hied,
Own April's music in their breast hath died,
And croft and copse resound not as before.
But, in this privileged Isle, this brave, this blest,
This deathless England, it seems always Spring.
Though graver wax the days, Song takes not wing.
In Autumn boughs it builds another nest :
Even from the snow we lift our hearts and sing.
And still your voice is heard above the rest.

A FRAGMENT

PART I

TO-DAY, and in this England! Wherefore not?
Shall the sepulchral yesterdays alone
Murmur of music, and our ears still lean
Toward sleeping stone for voices from the grave?
Back unto life, ye living! Nothing new
Under the sun? Say rather, nothing old.
Have the winds lost their freshness, or the Spring
One dimple of her beauty? Looks the moon,
Whom lovers will with tight-locked palms to-night
Gaze on in silence, by the silence hushed,
One hour less young than when, o'er Trojan plains,
To Trojan eyes, she shepherded the stars?
Hero's true lamp is out; Leander's arms
No longer breast the barricading surge;
But beckoning lights still burn in lonely breasts,
And seas of separation moan unseen
'Twixt love and locked embraces, salter far

Than e'er embittered sweet Abydos' shore.
Let Delphi's fire be quenched ; fresh vapours rise
From smouldering hollows in the human heart,
Propounding riddles only verse can read.
Who understand not, ne'er had understood.

"Sheds all its golden gains upon the ground,
Leaving itself quite bare !" Thus far, aloud,
Murmured Sir Alured, and then broke off,
Completing not his own mind's parallel.
For he was standing 'mid the smooth domain,
He newly called his own, his sire just dead,
And the year slowly dying, when his gaze
Paused at an ancient sycamore bereft
Of all its leaves, that lay upon the ground,
It black, they burnished, and had felt the shock
Of a too timely close comparison.
"Leaving itself quite bare !" again he sighed,
"Like the old arms of that too generous tree,
Whose latest, poorest, barest branch am I !"
Then strode he on, and gazed upon the earth,
As do we all when sadness with the soul
A silent parley holds, since that we know
Under the earth earth's sadness will be stilled.

Upon the crest, midway, of wooded ridge,
Stands brick-built Avoncourt, its feudal face
Set firmly toward the south, whose smile it takes
When smile is given ; but, when the skies are dim,
It wears on its indented front a look
Like battered armour.   Each fresh age hath striven
To keep it young and drape its rugged years
With gentler graces of the newer time.
Below the stone-girt terrace that recalls
Merlon and embrasure of sterner days,
Now softened down to peaceful purposes—
Peripatetic dialogue, or 'chance
The slow faint foot of some fair sentinel,
Who, since the voice she loves to list, not now
Murmurs unmeasured music in her ear,
Tells discreet night her secret and drinks in
The indefinite passion of the nightingale—
Stretch lake-like lawns, and islands of fair flowers.
Beyond, rolls wooded chase, where startled deer
With quick short jerks 'neath clean-lopped branches
        bound,
And in the bracken forest disappear,
Or upon open velvet spaces couched,
With antlers motionless and haunches sleek,

Consume the day in graceful idleness.
Its immemorial majesty of boughs
Shuts out the common world ; but should you stray
Past its exclusive precincts, you are lost,
Lost utterly in world of sprays and stems,
That ever and anon divide, and show
Long leafy cloisters where rapt silence prays
When no man's desecrating foot is there.

But though its woods, glades, pastures, still are
      fair,
Progress, that boastful spendthrift who eats up
The savings of the parsimonious Past,
Hath squandered all except its loveliness.
In time's fast growing legendary now,
When service was the other pole of sway,
On whose joint axis moved the duteous world,
The fief of Avoncourt was still alert
To furnish forth a knight, a horse, a shield,
And, on their feet, a modest retinue.
Then came the later and the laxer days,
When gentlehood, its armour doffing, stayed
Mildly at home, wielding a lazy rule,
And to poor mercenary starvelings left

The lists of honour.   With no foe to kill
Save time, who, killed, straight comes to life again,
Its desultory lords their lives despatched
'Twixt fox and flagon ; hunted, boozed, and slept,
More fatly fed and brawnier boors among
Big raw-boned boors, their brethren, who revered
With forelocks pulled a sceptre meaningless.
But when the New Age bustled into view,
And sleek evangelists with purse and scrip,
Converts to comfortable tenets, cried,
" Be rich and fear not !" and mankind received
The golden gospel with attentive ears,
And leaving father, mother, followed it,
Dominion's shadow slipped from Avoncourt.
It bore not, like the patriarch's spouse of old,
Within its womb a wonder late-conceived,
Such as in shires to north of Trent hath shed
On ostentatious plutocrats awhile
A counterfeited primacy which men
Will but to valorous wisdom long concede.
And so its race waxed insignificant ;
Under the waves of opulence submerged,
And, since contending with the mounting tide,
More deeply drowned.

           "A wealthy wife mends all.
Why not?   It is the custom of the time.
I loiter out of fashion."   As he spoke,
The staghound pacing gravely at his side
Gave a bound forward, and was suddenly lost.
He, freshly in his new-found thought entranced,
Walked on, and heeding not the truant hound,
Let the path lead him, till the cloistered woods
Closed all around him, and on autumn leaves
He trod, with autumn leaves above his head.
But when the dream of mercenary bed
Waxed unto vivid nightmare, and he woke,
Catching his breath and asking was it true,
"Lufra!" he called, whistled, and waiting stood.
And lo! from out an aisle-like avenue
Came Lufra, slow, and on her grizzled head
A hand of white and tapering tenderness,
The index of a form he quickly scanned,
Fresh as a bud that just hath burst its sheath,
A fragrant blossom of May maidenhood.
"I have lost my way among these woods," she gasped,
With a little laugh of shy perplexity,
And glancing round as though to run away,
Had she known where to run to.   "Much I fear,

I trespass, too." He taken unawares
By the sharp contrast betwixt sordid dream
And fair reality, quickly exclaimed
Ere taking thought, " It were a churlish wood,
A churlish world, that deemed you trespasser !
Where would you go?"

                           To maiden ear and heart
There nothing is in all the scale of sound
So sweet as unpremeditated praise ;
And he had lauded her unwittingly.
" I would go home ;" and therewithal she named
A cosy farm upon the southern verge
Of the land that called him lord, and told him how,
There mid the milk-sweet breath of homely kine,
Of cocks that crowed as though 'twere always dawn,
Of orchard-branches strung with coral fruit,
And porches cool with untrimmed honeysuckle,
She from the stale and stifling town had come,
To tend, as well as inexperience might,
Her mother's sister, only mother now.
" And may I be your guide?"—" You must," she
        said,
" Unless you mean me to go rudderless

Through this big wood which is to me a sea,
Whereof I have not got the chart ; its paths,
Like to the waves, into each other fall,
Perplexing in their uniformity.
Do they not puzzle you ?"—" Me ? No," he said,
" I, learned to thread them ere I learned that life
Hath any puzzles." Therewith walked they on,
Slim form by side of stalwart, mated well.
" Perhaps these woods are yours ?" she said. " They
  are.
Is it not sad ?" For she had led him back
By that home question to the thought wherewith
His mind had started. "Sad ?" she asked. " For
  whom ?
For you, or for the woods ?"—" Alas ! for both."
Quick glancing up, she noticed that his garb
Symbolised sorrow. " Sad, you mean, because
They fell to you but recently, and thus
Possession signifieth deeper loss."
" Aye, sad enough is that, but sadder still
When they who go but burden him that stays.
May we not doubt if stooping Atlas finds,
Too busy with his burden to look up,
The earth he shoulders, very beautiful.

The rivers roll above him, and the woods,
Leafier they are, the more they cumber him.
But look ! a shore to your bewildering sea."

And true, the pathway ended, stopped abrupt
By a gate that led into a field new-reaped,
Whereon were pheasants gleaning.   Here he leaned,
And she, because he was her guide, leaned too,
Gazing upon the scene, but he on her.
" How beautiful !" he murmured,—thinking of her ;
While she, unconscious of his theme, and rapt
All in the scene, " How beautiful !" replied :
" How peaceful !"   And the music of her voice
Made music and peace in his unpeaceful heart.

Earth, our reputed Mother, so we lend
Our souls to her familiar influence,
Wills not that any of her children be
To one another strangers ; and so close
Are we by instinct and dumb voice of blood,
That the harsh stepdame Custom ofttimes fails,
Even when girt with all its ceremony,
To keep us quite as alien as it would.
But when in lieu of jealous boundaries,

Of ambushed eyes, assassinating tongues,
And hearts expert in moral sophistry,
That from some lively premiss straight infer
Deadly conclusion, Nature's kindly troop,
The sky's ingenuous countenance, the frank,
The candid air, the unimputing woods,
The river flowing irresponsibly,
Make all our company, from them we draw
Contagious candour, and respond as free
As doth Æolian harp to hazard winds.

So, leaning there, with none to come between
The stirless autumn sunshine and their souls,
He, half to her, half to himself, resumed.
"Yes, they are mine, for that brief tenancy
Which we call life. We are but tenants all,
Despite pretentious parchments, and my sires,
Whom death hath ousted from this holding, held
Under a kindlier landlord, that lost time,
Which we are told we ne'er shall find again,
When days and nights were easy, and men's deeds
And duties travelled along well-worn grooves,
Impalpable, yet certain as the track
On which revolve the seasons. Now, alas!

All grows uncertain and irregular.
None serves, none sways.   We chaffer for our rights,
And haggle over service.   Which pays best,
We ask, where all pays badly,—till we learn
That unpaid duty is best paid of all."

She listened ; for believing youth that hears
Dark utterance, straight infers an oracle.
But he, aware he somewhat overmuch
Reflected autumn's abstract haziness,
Added, "Forgive me if I dreamed aloud,
And to a simple question gave you back
A round of riddles.   Yes, the woods are mine.
Should I not rather say that I am theirs?"

Thereat, with little skill and no device,
But in that homely speech which moves us more
Than all the tropes of foreign rhetoric,
She said the very happiest lot on earth,
To her at least it seemed, was thus to be
Lord of the soil in England's lovely isle.
"Aye, aye," he said, sharp interrupting her,
"Its loveliness we kill not all at once,
Though many a rood, once fair and profitless,

To profitable foulness hath been warped,
And Nature every year pays heavier tax,
To wear her native livery.   There you stand,
Rich in your youth, rich in your comeliness,
Their value undecreased by time or change ;
For comeliness and youth, ten æons hence,
Will be as young and comely and as prized
As they are now, while these poor woods will be
Burnt up to make some pandemonium puff
The smoke of Progress into Heaven's fixed face,
Or measured out in yards to serve as fringe
On thrifty Competition's narrow skirts.
Still they are mine, and I am theirs, and we
Must face the age together : cruel age,
Which makes men timid to be poor, withal
Still poorer, squandering life in dying rich."

" I thought the age we live in was," she said,
Still in response to scornful images
Tending the words of meek simplicity,
" Reputed great.   I ever hear it praised,
Called wiser, better, more intelligent
Than all its sires.   But I am ignorant
And only echo back the sounds I hear."

"We play with sounding words; men ever did :
It is not children only love the drum ;"
Again with ready gibe he answered her.
"Progress :—but whither?   Our contentions are
The wheels that carry Progress on its road.
But who is it that drives, and who that gains,
Because we still accelerate the pace?
The axles of our poor revolving selves
Grow hot and hotter and still muddier ;
But never one inch nearer comes the goal.
How should it, when no pocket compass shows
Whether we go to, or away from, it ?"

"God is the goal," she said, with reverent lips.
"Then being the goal, He must be stationary,
While we progress.   Do we progress towards Him ?
Do railways, or with broad or narrow gauge,
Bring us one station nearer unto Heaven ?
The electric leap, annihilating time,
As long as ever leaves Eternity ;
And all its boasted currents, speed as far
As e'er they can, bury themselves in earth,
And end their circuit where they started from."
Then, in a sadder tone, "O bootless round !

I do but see a motion meaningless,
With its monotonous mutability.
The years are linked to years, a lengthening chain ;
But the hours wax not brighter, nor the days
Longer, nor yet the seasons fuller of hope."

"How sad you make the autumn afternoon !
And yet I cannot gladden it," she said.
"But others might, and, doing it, would plead
That Progress truer triumphs has to show
Than these, material, mechanical,
That leave us matter still.   Does thought not move ?"
"It moves," he answered, "just as ocean moves,
Backward and forward ; but its bulk remains
Long while unchanged, as do its boundaries.
Like architecture, thought would seem to have ta'en
All forms already that are possible.
Nought new is said, but only newly vamped ;
And these pretentious novelties wherein
The upstart age struts proudly, are but gems
Carefully carven by an olden time,
Some cunning hand hath furbished up anew
And furnished with fresh setting."—"That sounds
      true,"

Gaining contentious courage, she replied :
" But metaphors well-chosen always do."
" Life is itself a metaphor," he said,
" Full of ambiguous meaning, striving still
To represent a something that is not.
We cannot get behind ourselves.   Thus, he
Who stands at the meridian of life,
Will count as much enlightenment behind
As in the future he anticipates.
The eye whose sun is setting deems mankind
Hath run its course of wisdom ; while the boy,
Since just out of his cradle, never doubts
That History backward is as dark as night,
And that the sunshine of the waking world
Is all to come.   All partial, and all, false.
If this be sad, then life hath little joy."

" Meanwhile we make no progress to *my* goal,"
She said with a smile.   So through the gate they
       passed,
Across the crackling stubble, onward thence
Over reaped aftermaths, bright emeralds set
In golden ring of autumn's circling woods ;
Over rude stile, with help of stronger hand,

First touch of palms whereby the spirit will oft
Send half-obscure electric messages,
Deciphered later.

PART II

" Loved me ? Hath love a past then ? What is that,
Once love, now love no longer ? . . . Boastful fool !
Who is the victor now ? These empty hands,
These empty halls, declare it, and I range
With farewell feet ancestral corridors,
With echo for my servitor. . . . Violet eyes,
And hair like sheaves of sunshine ; eyebrows broad,
Matching the tresses, arched, but outlined strong—
Not baby stencillings—'neath which, at times,
Broadened a gaze that seemed as looking out
Of all the Past at all Futurity.
Small dainty hands, as soft as captured bird,
So soft, we fear to crush it !—soft and white,
With feet to mate, fantastically fine,
True hint of her perfection, promised mine,
Now pawned another's for a sordid gain,
And ne'er to be redeemed ! O' roof despised,
Withal so proud, that might have sheltered both,

K

And now must shelter neither, house thy ghosts,
My ancestors, and what I might have been,
Had woman's faith been fixed ! Now all things slip,
Past, present, future, down the gulf of time,
That whelms not me, who need must ride aloft
Upon its eddy, a still whirling leaf,
Too trivial to drown !

Part III

Deep thickets of green silence. For it was
A summer noon, and summer was asleep,
And lent them welcome, but beheld them not.
Only themselves, and stillness, and the sweet
Shelter of interpenetrating boughs,
And bracken thick and footfalls unreturned
From the deep soft dry sheddings of the pine.

Deep down into her lucid eyes he gazed,
And clear he saw his image quivering there,
The shadow of his gazing and his thought.
For she was like a snow-fed lake that draws
Into its bosom only high-born streams ;
And he was like a cloudless night whose day

Has been the battlefield of clashing storms,
Raging, retreating, and returning still.
But now below the horizon were they gone,
And on her upward soul downward he shone,
With the serenity of a silent star.

A WILD ROSE

I

THE first wild rose in wayside hedge,
    This year I wandering see,
I pluck, and send it as a pledge,
    My own Wild Rose, to Thee.

II

For when my gaze first met thy gaze,
    We were knee-deep in June :
The nights were only dreamier days,
    And all the hours in tune.

III

I found thee, like the eglantine,
    Sweet, simple, and apart ;
And, from that hour, thy smile hath been
    The flower that scents my heart.

IV

And, ever since, when tendrils grace
   Young copse or weathered bole
With rosebuds, straight I see thy face,
   And gaze into thy soul.

V

A natural bud of love Thou art,
   Where, gazing down, I view,
Deep hidden in thy fragrant heart,
   A drop of heavenly dew.

VI

Go, wild rose, to my Wild Rose dear ;
   Bid her come swift and soon.
O would that She were always here !
   It then were always June.

GLEANERS OF FAME

HEARKEN not, friend, for the resounding din
That did the Poet's verses once acclaim :
We are but gleaners in the field of fame,
Whence the main harvest hath been gathered in.
The sheaves of glory you are fain to win,
Long since were stored round many a household
    name,
The reapers of the Past, who timely came,
And brought to end what none can now begin.
Yet, in the stubbles of renown, 'tis right
To stoop and gather the remaining ears,
And carry homeward in the waning light
What hath been left us by our happier peers ;
So that, befall what may, we be not quite
Famished of honour in the far-off years.

Printed by R. & R. CLARK, *Edinburgh.*

POETICAL WORKS

BY THE SAME AUTHOR.

Crown 8vo. 10s. 6d.

THE HUMAN TRAGEDY.

Crown 8vo. 3s. 6d.

MADONNA'S CHILD.

[*Which, though part of ' The Human Tragedy,' can be had separately*.]

Crown 8vo. 9s.

THE TOWER OF BABEL.

Crown 8vo. 5s.

INTERLUDES.

Crown 8vo. 5s.

THE GOLDEN AGE.

Crown 8vo. 5s.

THE SEASON.

WILLIAM BLACKWOOD AND SONS:
EDINBURGH AND LONDON.

———

Crown 8vo. 7s. 6d.

SAVONAROLA.

Crown 8vo. 6s.

SOLILOQUIES IN SONG.

Crown 8vo. 6s.

AT THE GATE OF THE CONVENT.

Crown 8vo. 6s.

PRINCE LUCIFER.

———

MACMILLAN AND CO., LONDON.

MACMILLAN AND CO.'S PUBLICATIONS.

Matthew Arnold's Complete Poetical Works. New Edition, with Additional Poems. Three Vols. Crown 8vo. 7s. 6d. each. Vol. I. Early Poems, Narrative Poems, and Sonnets. Vol. II. Lyric and Elegiac Poems. Vol. III. Dramatic and Later Poems.

Charles Kingsley's Complete Poetical Works. New Edition, with Additional Poems.
EVERSLEY EDITION. Two Vols. Globe 8vo. 10s.
UNIFORM EDITION. One Vol. Crown 8vo. 6s.
POPULAR EDITION. One Vol. Crown 8vo. 3s. 6d. *[Just ready.*

Charles Lamb's Plays, Poems, and Miscellaneous Essays. Edited, with Introduction and Notes, by the Rev. ALFRED AINGER, Canon of Bristol. Globe 8vo. 5s.

Ralph Waldo Emerson's Poems. Globe 8vo. 5s.

The Poems of Arthur Hugh Clough. New Edition. Crown 8vo. 7s. 6d.

Poems. By STOPFORD A. BROOKE, M.A. Globe 8vo. 6s.

Riquet of the Tuft: a Love Drama. By the same Author. Extra crown 8vo. 6s.

By GEORGE MEREDITH.

Poems and Lyrics of the Joy of Earth. Extra fcap. 8vo. 6s.
Ballads and Poems of Tragic Life. Extra fcap. 8vo. 6s.
A Reading of Earth. Extra fcap. 8vo. 5s.

By F. W. H. MYERS, M.A.

The Renewal of Youth, and other Poems. Crown 8vo. 7s. 6d.
St. Paul. A Poem. New Edition. Extra fcap. 8vo. 2s. 6d.

By ERNEST MYERS.

The Puritans. A Poem. Extra fcap. 8vo. 2s. 6d.
Poems. Extra fcap. 8vo. 4s. 6d.
The Defence of Rome, and other Poems. Extra fcap. 8vo. 5s.
The Judgment of Prometheus, and other Poems. Extra fcap. 8vo. 3s. 6d.

By CHRISTINA ROSSETTI.

Poems. Complete Edition. With Four Illustrations. Extra fcap. 8vo. 6s.
A Pageant, and other Poems. Extra fcap. 8vo. 6s.

MACMILLAN AND CO., LONDON.

www.ingramcontent.com/pod-product-compliance
Lightning Source LLC
Chambersburg PA
CBHW031121020726
47495CB00007B/2290